Level 4 is ideal for children w
read longer stories with a wider
are eager to start reading indep

Special features:

Clear type
Full, exciting story
Richer, more varied vocabulary

Once there was a little mermaid who lived under the sea with her father and her older sisters.

Like all mermaids, she had a beautiful tail and a beautiful voice.

6

7

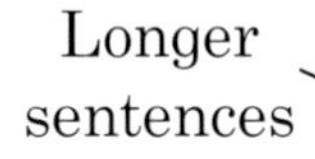
Longer sentences

Detailed illustrations capture the imagination

The little mermaid went back to watch the prince again and again.

But she knew that humans did not love mermaids. And she knew she could not live on land with her tail.

She wished she could be human, so she could be with the prince.

22

23

Educational Consultant: Geraldine Taylor
Book Banding Consultant: Kate Ruttle

A catalogue record for this book is available from the British Library

Published by Ladybird Books Ltd
80 Strand, London, WC2R 0RL
A Penguin Company

001

ISBN: 978-0-72328-070-5

Printed in China

The Little Mermaid

Retold by Ronne Randall
Illustrated by Milly Teggle

Once there was a little mermaid who lived under the sea with her father and her older sisters.

Like all mermaids, she had a beautiful tail and a beautiful voice.

The little mermaid was not old enough to go up above the water and see the land, but her sisters were. They told her they had seen humans there – people who walked on two legs.

The little mermaid wanted to see the people, too.

At last, the little mermaid was old enough to go up above the water.

She saw a ship, and on the ship was a handsome young prince. As soon as she saw him, the little mermaid fell in love with him.

All at once a storm came up. The prince's ship turned over in the waves. The prince was hurt, and he fell into the water.

"I have to help him!" said the little mermaid.

The little mermaid took the prince to the shore. She stayed with him until the storm was over.

When the prince opened his eyes, he saw the little mermaid looking down at him.

But the little mermaid saw people coming to help, so she swam away.

The little mermaid told her sisters that she was in love with the handsome young prince.

One of her sisters knew where the prince lived. “I can take you there,” she said.

The little mermaid went with her sister to see the prince's palace. She watched the prince as he walked by the shore.

The little mermaid went back to watch the prince again and again.

But she knew that humans did not love mermaids. And she knew she could not live on land with her tail.

She wished she could be human, so she could be with the prince.

The little mermaid was very sad. At last her sisters said, "Go to the old sea witch. She can help you."

"I love a human prince," the little mermaid told the witch. "Can you make me human, so I can be with him on land?"

"There is a potion that will turn your tail into legs," said the witch, "but it will take away your voice. It will only come back if the prince loves you. Do you want the potion?"

"Yes," said the little mermaid.

"When you take this potion, you will go to sleep," the witch told the little mermaid. "When you wake up, your tail will be gone and you will have legs."

The little mermaid swam to the prince's palace. She took the witch's potion and fell asleep.

When she woke up, her tail was gone and she had two legs.

Soon the prince came down to the shore and saw the little mermaid.

"You look like a girl who saved me when I was hurt in a storm," he said. "Are you that girl?"

But the little mermaid could not talk – her voice was gone.

The prince said the little mermaid could come and stay in his palace.

"I wish you could tell me who you are," he said. But the little mermaid could not, and she could not tell him that she loved him.

One day, a beautiful princess came to the palace.

The little mermaid watched the prince walking and talking with the princess. The prince looked happy, but the little mermaid was sad.

"My father wants me to marry the princess," the prince told the little mermaid. "But the only girl I want to marry is the one who saved me in the storm."

The prince went to walk by the sea. The little mermaid went, too.

When the prince turned and saw the little mermaid, he saw that her eyes were full of love.

All at once the prince knew who she was!

"You are the girl who saved me!" said the prince. "You are the girl I love! Will you marry me?"

"Yes," said the little mermaid. The prince loved her at last, and she had her voice back.

They were married that very day. The little mermaid and the prince were so happy.

The little mermaid could see her sisters waving to her out at sea. They were also happy for their little sister and her handsome young prince.

How much do you remember about the story of The Little Mermaid? Answer these questions and find out!

- Who does the little mermaid live with?
- Who does the little mermaid fall in love with?
- Who do the sisters tell the little mermaid to go and see?
- What does the sea witch give to the little mermaid?
- Why can't the little mermaid talk to the prince?
- How does the little mermaid get her voice back?

Unjumble these words to make words from the story, then match them to the correct pictures.

rnceip   het telitl iadmemr

caalpe   gsle   ichtw

Read it yourself with Ladybird

Tick the books you've read!

For more confident readers who can read simple stories with help.

Level
3
YOU won't like this present as much as I DO!
The Elves and the Shoemaker
Hansel and Gretel
Harry and the Bucketful of Dinosaurs
Jack and the Beanstalk
The Red Knight
Furi on Music Island
Poppet Stows Away
Rapunzel
Aladdin
The Jungle Book
Roxy and the Great Escape
ANGRY BIRDS CHEER UP, CHUCK!
ANGRY BIRDS BOMB'S BEST BIRTHDAY

Longer stories for more independent, fluent readers.

Level
4
I am Inventing an INVENTION
Harry and the Dinosaurs United
Heidi
Katsuma and the Art Thief
Luvli and the Glump-a-tron
The Pied Piper of Hamelin
Sam and the Robots
Snow White and the Seven Dwarfs
The Wizard of Oz
The Little Mermaid
Alice in Wonderland
Oddie The Hero
ANGRY BIRDS RED AND THE GREAT FUNG OFF
ANGRY BIRDS